W9-ACD-384

Kitaq

Goes Ice Fishing

•

Story by

Margaret Nicolai

Paintings by

David Rubin

•

ALASKA NORTHWEST BOOKS™

Anchorage • Seattle • Portland

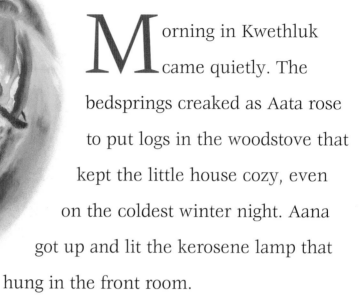

Morning in Kwethluk
came quietly. The
bedsprings creaked as Aata rose
to put logs in the woodstove that
kept the little house cozy, even
on the coldest winter night. Aana
got up and lit the kerosene lamp that
hung in the front room.

In bed, crowded with his two older brothers, little Kitaq
began to stir. Today was a special day. His grandfather,
Apa'urluk, was coming to visit, and maybe today he would take
Kitaq fishing in the ice. Quietly, Kitaq crawled from beneath
the warm blankets. He pulled on his moose-hide slippers and
padded into the main room of the house.

"Good morning, Son," said his mother with a smile. "You are up early today."

"Yes, Aana," he said. "Apa'urluk is coming, and maybe I will go fishing in the ice with him."

His father chuckled. "Apa will take you fishing when you are big enough to walk all the way there and all the way back. You must be old enough not to cry when your feet are cold and tired."

"Oh I am, Aata," Kitaq said with pride. "I can walk all the way to the store and back with Aana, and I am never tired."

"We'll see," said Aata, winking at Aana. "It is much farther to the fishing holes than it is to the store."

Kitaq's mother served his father coffee and set a plate of pancakes on the table. Every morning she cooked round, brown pancakes on a hot griddle on top of the woodstove. Kitaq could eat many of his mother's pancakes, each of which he rolled up and dunked into a small bowl of sugar next to his plate.

The house was quiet, except for the sounds of father and son eating breakfast and the crackling of the fire in the stove. The scent of the coffee hung in the air, and the room glowed yellow with the light from the kerosene lamp.

As he reached for another pancake, Kitaq heard the *crunch-crunch* of footsteps outside in the cold, dry snow. Then *stomp-stomp* on the porch and a creak as the outer door opened. As soon as his grandfather appeared in the doorway, Kitaq raced to his side.

"Apa, I am big now. Today will you take me fishing in the ice?"

"Son, you must let Apa in, and let him take off his *atkuk* (parka)," said Aana gently.

Kitaq remembered that young people did not address elders unless spoken to. He looked down at the floor and went back to the table. He watched as Apa took off his *aliimatik* (gloves) and pulled his *atkuk* over his head. Grandfather sat on a chair next to Kitaq, while Aana brought coffee and another plate for pancakes.

"You are up early today, Kitaq," his grandfather said with a wink. "Yes, Apa, I am awake because I knew you were coming, and I hoped you might take me fishing with you. I think I can walk all the way to the ice holes and all the way back, and I will not cry when my feet are cold and tired."

"Well, Grandson, let me eat and visit. Then we will talk about fishing."

Kitaq nodded patiently and quietly finished his breakfast. His two brothers and two sisters were beginning to wake up. After breakfast, they walked the path to school. Next fall, when he was six, Kitaq would join them.

To show how big he was, Kitaq struggled into his layers of winter clothes. His fingers were still clumsy with the buttons on his flannel shirt and the socks he pulled on were different colors, but he was proud to dress himself.

Apa had finished eating and visiting. Kitaq slid next to his grandfather at the table. He had been so patient that he was ready to burst.

"So, Grandson, you think that you can walk all the way to the ice holes and all the way back, and that your feet would not be cold or tired?"

"Oh, yes!" Kitaq said. "I think I could do that."

"Very well, you may go fishing with me today."

Only big boys went fishing with Apa. Kitaq swelled with pride and his face split wide in a smile. His feet wiggled in a little dance and he threw his arms around Apa.

"Ask your mother to pack your lunch, and I will go for the sled. When I come back, we will go fishing," Apa said, returning Kitaq's hug with smiling eyes. He left the house with a chuckle, shaking his head at his grandson's excitement.

Kitaq watched Aana put dried fish and meat, some fried bread, a candy bar, and a drink into his *atmak* (backpack).

When he heard Apa's steps in the snow, Kitaq was dressed and ready. He was out the door even before Apa opened it.

"I am ready now," he said. "We can go fishing."

"I see that you are ready, Grandson. Did you tell your mother good-bye and remember your lunch?" asked his grandfather.

"Everything is here in the pack. And Aana is waving to us through the window. We are all ready to go fishing."

Kitaq led the way as Apa pulled the sled along the path beside the river. "Slow down, Grandson. The fish will wait for us. It is a long way. If you hurry, you will be tired," cautioned Apa.

Kitaq sighed and slowed down for a few steps, then began to walk quickly again. Above the horizon, the sun had risen, but it was still cold. Small puffs of breath circled Kitaq's head as he walked.

After a while, Kitaq's footsteps slowed. The breaths came faster from his mouth as he trudged down the path. He could see the corner where they would turn and walk down the steep bank to the river. He knew the fishing holes were just beyond. Although they had walked for some time, the corner was still far away.

Kitaq felt a little tired, but the thought of a fish on the line kept his feet going along the path, one in front of the other. Finally they reached the corner, and stepped down the bank and onto the thick ice over the river.

Tall sticks marked the ice holes. Kitaq handed Apa the ice pick from the sled so he could break the new ice that had formed in the fishing hole. Next to the hole, Kitaq helped spread an old moose hide to kneel on. Using a dull metal ladle, Apa scooped the slush and ice chunks floating in the water inches from the opening of the hole. Kitaq handed his grandfather the fishing poles and the small bag of dried salmon eggs for bait.

"Are you ready to fish?" Apa asked, as he unwound the strings from the poles. Then he slid eggs onto the hooks and handed Kitaq a pole.

As he knelt by the hole, Kitaq gently lowered his hook. He leaned over and peered through the brown water, trying to see the fish swimming in the water below. The ice was three feet deep and silty, with a fresh white layer of snow on top.

Kitaq chewed his lip as he bobbed the string just so. The string was taut, and he felt the current gently pull the line. First a nibble, then a sharp tug nearly jerked the pole from his hands.

"Apa, a fish!" shouted Kitaq. He jumped up and pulled hard on the line. Out from the ice came his beautiful silvery fish. It flopped about and almost fell back into the hole.

"You have done well, Grandson. This big *luqruuyak* (pike) will feed your whole family for dinner." Apa pulled the hook from the pike's mouth and slid the fish near the sled.

Kitaq could hardly wait to lower his hook again. This time the fish made him wait a bit longer, but soon he felt another nibble and tug. In all, Kitaq caught three fish before his grandfather told him to stop and come eat by the fire he had made on the bank. Reluctantly, he left the hole and sat on a log to eat lunch. All that fishing made him hungry and he ate quickly.

"You may fish just a while longer, then we must go back. It is a long walk, and the day is short now," Apa said to Kitaq, who raced back to the hole to fish again.

Kitaq sat bobbing the string, waiting and waiting. He knew that his grandfather was repacking the sled, and soon they would have to leave. This time the fish were not hungry.

"We must go now, Grandson."

"But Apa, I know another fish will bite soon," pleaded Kitaq.

"It is time to go now," Apa said.

The tone of his grandfather's voice reminded Kitaq that his mother had told him he must obey Apa, and he turned sadly from the hole in the ice. He wrapped the string around the pole and tucked it under the cover of the sled. Then he climbed up to the path. Behind him he heard Apa straining to get the sled up the tall bank. He looked back as his grandfather topped the hill and then he started on the path to home.

"It is a special day when a boy catches his first fish," Apa said as they walked. "It means that now he can help feed the family. You must share your first catch. Mother will prepare a feast for the family and friends. It will be a celebration feast for you."

Kitaq nodded, and he lifted his chin with pride, but he was too tired to answer. He had used up all his energy on fishing, and now the walk home was too long. His steps slowed until he stopped.

"I am tired, Apa. I need to rest," he said wearily. "I cannot walk another step."

"Then we will stop for just a minute," Apa said. "The sun is close to the ground now, and soon it will be gone. We must get home before the sky is dark."

Kitaq sank onto the snow near the path. "I wish we were home now," he quavered.

Apa laid his hand on Kitaq's shoulder and gave a gentle squeeze. "I know you are tired, Grandson. You have walked all the way to the fishing holes, you caught fish, and now it is a long walk home. If you stand up and take one step at a time, we will be home soon."

One tear ran down Kitaq's cheek. He was weary all the way through to his bones. He rubbed the tear away with his mitten.

"Come on now, Kitaq," Apa said. "We must go. If you get too tired, just step on the runners of the sled and I will pull you."

Kitaq got behind the sled as Apa put his shoulders into the rope harness. For a short time, Kitaq pushed the sled and Apa felt the rope go slack. Then when he became too tired, Kitaq stepped on the runners and rested his head against the bar. The rope harness tightened and Apa felt the weight of Kitaq's small body. As he pulled the tired fisherman toward the lights of the village, Apa smiled.

As he walked, Apa remembered his first fish, caught when he was a boy, more than sixty years ago. Many fish followed, but none was as special as the first. He remembered, too, his joy and pride as he served the fish to his own grandfather during his feast. Thinking of his tired grandson who napped on the runners of the sled, he felt the same pride.

Though the sun was nearly gone and the moon shone in the twilight, it was only late afternoon when Apa pulled the sled up to Kitaq's house. He shrugged off the harness, then gently shook his sleeping grandson.

"Wake up, Grandson, and tell your mother of your success. I will bring the fish to show her."

Aana was watching from the window as the fishermen returned. She opened the door.

"Aana, I caught three fish," said Kitaq proudly.

Aana looked at the fish, smiled, and hugged Kitaq. "Look at these! We will make a fine soup from them for a feast of celebration. You are a fisherman now."

Warmed by Aana's praise, Kitaq came in and took off his outdoor clothes. His feet were cold, so he sat and wiggled them near the stove. He was glad to be home in the cozy house. As Aana cut the fish for soup, Kitaq looked out at the darkening sky. He went to Apa, who sat at the table drinking coffee.

"Thank you for taking me fishing, Apa," Kitaq said almost shyly.

"You walked a long way, Grandson. You walked all the way there. You caught three fish and walked most of the way back. Today was a special day for both of us. I am glad you are my grandson."

Kitaq put his arms around Apa and gave him a big hug. He listened to the good, warm hissing of the soup pot and the cheerful humming of his mother as she cooked. He snugged his cheek to Grandfather's chest and heard the beating of his heart.

Soon the rest of Kitaq's family would come home, and they would help prepare the celebration feast. Aunts, uncles, cousins, and friends would be invited to come and share Kitaq's fish. The little house would be filled with happy people, but none as happy as Kitaq.

About the Yup'ik Village of Kwethluk

Kitaq's stories are fictional accounts of stories my husband, Matthew, tells of his experiences growing up Kwethluk, Alaska, in the 1950s-60s. At that time Kwethluk's population was about 300 people, almost all Yup'ik Eskimos (The "Genuine" People). Today Kwethluk's population is about 500 people. Located on the Kwethluk River, approximately 12 air miles from Bethel, it is the largest village in southwest Alaska. Bethel is connected to Anchorage, almost 400 miles away, with regular airline flights and small plane flights to every village in the region. All villages in this remote region are accessible only by air or river travel.

Rivers are the lifeline of the Yup'ik people. In the summer, boats travel up and down the Kwethluk River, leaving white wakes in sluggish brown water. When winter freezes the ice 5 to 6 feet deep, the river becomes a highway for cars, trucks, and snowmobiles, where not long ago dog sleds and foot power were common.

Village life is much the same now as it was in my husband's youth. Yup'iks still live a subsistence lifestyle. They depend on the river for their major food source: salmon that travel from the ocean up the winding rivers each summer. Wild game is also harvested: moose, bear, caribou, reindeer, as well as small game.

A village store carries everything from groceries to gasoline. Its goods are shipped along the river on barges during the short summer. Now, supplies also arrive on small airplanes that land daily at the dusty dirt airstrip alongside the village. Limited access raises prices and makes goods scarce. Since long before it became popular, Yup'iks have "recycled" by using and reusing everything possible.

Children attend the village school, where grades 1 through 12 are all housed in the same building. Each grade may have as few as five or as many as ten students, and several grades share classroom space. Until recently, most teachers came from the outside world, experiencing village life for the first time. Many qualified Yup'iks are returning to live and teach in the village now.

Villagers live in houses built on stilts to accommodate the shifting permafrost and the river that often spills over its banks in springtime. Electricity made its way into homes in the 1960s. However, homes are still without running water or plumbing. Water is hauled from a community well, and "honey buckets" are used instead of toilets. Many homes still use woodstoves for cooking and as their primary heat source. Telephones became common in the mid-1970s, and broadcast television soon followed.

Family is very important to Yup'ik culture. Elders are respected for their wisdom and experience, children are treasured and indulged. Yup'iks can trace the tangled family ties through the past generations to the present. It seems that everyone is related somehow.

Kwethluk, like most small Alaskan villages, is a close-knit community that looks after its own. Community spirit and cooperation are essential to survival in rural Alaska.

It's easy to sit on the riverbank in Kwethluk on a warm summer day and forget that the outside world exists. The tundra is painted a hundred shades of green, the air is clean and fresh, and the world feels new. Returning to Kwethluk for frequent visits from our home in Anchorage helps our family keep in touch with our village roots. When we go there, it's like traveling back in time 30 or 40 years. We are lucky to be able to share these Yup'ik Eskimo roots with our children, and I am proud to share them with you.

About the Author

Margaret Nicolai originally wrote Kitaq's (pronounced git-AWK) story as a Christmas present for her husband, Matthew. It was also written to preserve the story for her three children. Although her family lives in the city (Anchorage, Alaska), it is important to her that their children acknowledge and embrace their Yup'ik heritage.

Margaret is a full-time mom and a busy volunteer. She has spent many years volunteering with Girl Scouting. Recently, she was recognized as Outstanding Volunteer by the Anchorage School District for her support and service to the reading programs at Spring Hill School, where her children attend.

Her love of reading and children's literature, combined with her desire to preserve her husband's Yup'ik culture, have led to the publication of her first children's book, *Kitaq Goes Ice Fishing*.

About the Artist

Born in the Bronx, New York, artist David Rubin has lived in Alaska since his arrival in 1983. His formal art training included study at the Art Student's League in New York and attendance at the Reilly League of Artists in White Plains, New York. The images he painted for this book are oil on canvas.

Since coming to Alaska, David has become an art instructor at the University of Alaska Southeast and exhibits his landscapes and portraits at several galleries in Alaska. He is also an accomplished musician and plays music in a local rock 'n' roll band called the Potlatch Band.

David has a Siberian Yup'ik daughter, Adrian Davina, and lives with her in Ketchikan.

Yup'ik Glossary

Aana (aa-NA) ∼ Mother

Aata (aa-TA) ∼ Father

aliimatik (a-lee-MUT-ik) ∼ mittens or gloves

Apa'urluk (up-AWR-u-look) ∼ Grandfather, (*Apa* ∼ familiar)

atkuk (ut-GOOK) ∼ parka, usually pullover, made from skins

atmuk (UT-muk) ∼ backpack or knapsack

kameksak (gum-UK-sak) ∼ Native-made, ankle-high fur boots

luqruuyak (luk-HOY-yuk) ∼ pike

To Matthew, David, Anya, and Eliana with love
—M.N.

To Adrian Davina, Gum-Gum, *a real Eskimo princess*
—D.R.

Text copyright © 1998 Margaret Nicolai
Illustrations copyright © 1998 David Rubin

Library of Congress Cataloging-in-Publication Data
Nicolai, Margaret, 1962–
      Kitaq goes ice fishing / by Margaret Nicolai; illustrations by David Rubin.
            p.   cm.
      Summary: Kitaq is not yet six years old when his grandfather takes him ice
fishing for the first time, carrying on a long-lived tradition among the Yupik people.
      ISBN 0-88240-504-7
      1. Yupik Eskimos—Juvenile fiction.   [1. Yupik Eskimos—Fiction.
2. Eskimos—Fiction. 3. Grandfathers—fiction. 4. Ice fishing—Fiction. 5. Fishing—
Fiction.]   I. Rubin, David, 1952–   ill.   II. Title.
PZ7.N55935Ki   1998   98-17335
[E]—dc21   CIP
                                                                          AC

Editor: Marlene Blessing
Managing Editor: Ellen Wheat
Designer: Constance Bollen

Alaska Northwest Books™
An imprint of Graphic Arts Center Publishing Company
P.O. Box 10306, Portland, OR 97296-0306
800-452-3032

Printed on acid-free and chlorine-free paper in Singapore